BEHAVIORAL ECONOMIC THEORY

JOHN LOK

ISBN 979-888569579-4

2020 Jan. Print Published

Contents

Preface

Introduction

What are our social customer and economic problems usually we will encounter in our lives. Can economists apply any economic theories to attempt to solve any economic or customer problems absolutely? Do economists apply any economic theories to solve any problems in any economic environment or situations or they need find the suitable economic theories to solve the suitable environment of economic or customer problems?

In my this book final chapter, I shall attempt to indicate some customer problems in electronic commerce strategy aspect and I shall explain how to apply economic theories to solve online consumers buying problem. I hope my readers can learn how and why economic theories can be the best strategy to solve e-commerce customer problems in e-commerce industry.

Prologue

Table of content

CHAPTER ONE

How applying economy theories solve economic problems

The economic problem – sometimes called the basic or central economic problem – asserts that an economy's finite resources are insufficient to satisfy all human wants and needs. Economics involves the study of how to allocate resources in conditions of scarcity However, viewing economics as the study of how society allocates resources can lead to conflation of normative economic planning and empirical study of how economic agents operate in these conditions.

In mainstream neoclassical economics, it is assumed that humans pursue their self-interest, and that the market mechanism best satisfies the various wants different individuals might have. These wants are often divided into individual wants (which depend on the individual's preferences and purchasing power parity) and collective wants (which are the wants of entire groups of people). Things such as food and clothing can be classified as either wants or needs, depending on what type and how often a good is requested.

However, economists have sometimes characterized "how" to produce as a "technological problem" of efficiency whereas the allocation of what is produced is an "economic problem". In a free market, the "how" of production and allocation of resources is distributed among economic agents. In a centrally planned economy, a principal decides how and what to produce on behalf of agents. Modern economies are often welfare capitalist with various regulations, which makes the economic system more equitable while retaining the distributed free market system. Due to human wants are unlimited, an infinite series of human wants remains continue with human life. Nobody can claim that all of his wants have been satisfied and he has no need to satisfy any further want. Everybody feels hunger at a time then other he needs water. Sometime one feels the desire of clothing then starts to feel the desire of having good conveyance. When all existing wants are satisfied then new wants starts to create in mind, so the series of wants remains continue till the last moment of life. So an economic problem arises because of existence of unlimited human wants.

- Problem of allocation of resources

The problem of allocation of resources arises due to the scarcity of resources, and refers to the question of which wants should be satisfied and which should be left unsatisfied. In other words, what to produce and how much to produce. More production of a good implies more resources required for the production of that good, and resources are scarce. These two facts together mean that, if a society decides to increase production of some good, it has to withdraw some resources from the production of other goods. In other words, more production of a desired commodity can be made possible only by reducing the quantity of resources used in the production of other goods.

The problem of allocation deals with the question of whether to produce capital goods or consumer goods. If the community decides to produce capital goods, resources must be withdrawn from the production of consumer goods. In the long run, however, [investment] in capital goods augments the production of consumer goods. Thus, both capital and consumer goods are important. The problem is determining the optimal production ratio between the two.

In fact, in our societies, resources are scarce and it is important to use them as efficiently as possible. Thus, it is essential to know if the production and distribution of national product made by an economy is maximally efficient. The production becomes efficient only if the productive resources are utilized in such a way that any reallocation does not produce more of one good without reducing the output of any other good. In other words, efficient distribution means that redistributing goods cannot make anyone better off without making someone else worse off. (See Pareto efficiency.) So, scientists will apply efficient distribution methods to help any countries to earn the absolute advantages when we buy and sell any kinds of products or food between ourselves countries, e.g. when US has good natural resource to grow any food, e.g. potato, wheat , vegetable, cotton , then

US can export to sell to China, because China has no any farms to grow agriculture food to supply itself Chinese to eat. So, China must need to buy any agriculture food from US. Otherwise, China has cheap labor to supply to US any manufacturers to help them to manufacture their electronic products. SO, it has many US factories are built in China to let Chinese workers help them to produce their products because their wages are cheaper to compare US workers. So, comparative economic advantage will be choice to apply between US and China both countries. (Absolute advantage trade theory)

The inefficiencies of production and distribution exist in all types of economies. The welfare of the people can be increased if these inefficiencies are ruled out. Some cost must be incurred to remove these inefficiencies. If the cost of removing these inefficiencies of production and distribution is more than the gain, then it is not worthwhile to remove them.

● The problem of full employment of resources

In view of how to use available resources are fully utilized is an important one. A community should achieve maximum satisfaction by using the scarce resources in the best possible manner—not wasting resources or using them inefficiently. There are two types of employment of resources:

(1) Labour-intensive

(2) Capital-intensive

In capitalist economies, however, available resources are not fully used. In times of depression, many people want to work but can't find employment. It supposes that the scarce resources are not fully utilized in a capitalistic economy.

● The problem of economic growth

If productive capacity grows, an economy can produce progressively more goods, which raises the standard of living. The increase in productive capacity of an economy is called economic growth. There are various factors affecting economic growth. The problems of economic growth have been discussed by numerous growth models, including the Harrod-Domar model, the neoclassical growth models of Solow and Swan, and the Cambridge growth models of Kaldor and Joan Robinson. This part of the economic problem is studied in the economies of development.

● Needs and wants problems

Needs are things or material items of peoples need for survival, such as food, clothing, housing, and water. Everyone has a different needs and wants. Until the Industrial Revolution, the vast majority of the world's population struggled for access to basic human needs.
Wants are effective desires for a particular product, or for something that can only be obtained by working for it. While the fundamental needs of survival are key in the function of the economy, wants are the driving force that stimulates demand for goods and services. To curb the economic problem, economists must classify the nature and different wants of consumers, as well as prioritize wants and organize production to satisfy as many wants as possible.

- Five bases problems of economy

In our societies , in general, our societies will have these similar problems The following points highlight the five basic problems of an economy. The problems are: 1. What to Produce and in What Quantities? 2. How to Produce these Goods? 3. For whom is the Goods Produced? 4. How Efficiently are the Resources being utilized? 5. Is the Economy Growing?.

Problem 1:What to Produce and in What Quantities?
The first central problem of an economy is to decide what goods and services are to be produced and in what quantities. This involves allocation of scarce resources in relation to the composition of total output in the economy. Since resources are scarce, the society has to decide about the goods to be produced: wheat, cloth, roads, television, power, buildings, and so on. Once the nature of goods to be produced is decided, then their quantities are to be decided. How many tones of wheat, how many televisions, how many million of power, how many buildings, etc. Since the resources of the economy are scarce, the problem of the nature of goods and their quantities has to be decided on the basis of priorities or preferences of the society.
If the society gives priority to the production of more consumer goods now, it will have less in the future. A higher priority on capital goods implies less consumer goods now and more in the future. But since resources are scarce, if some goods are produced in larger quantities, some other goods will have to be produced in smaller quantities. Suppose the economy produces capital goods and consumer goods. In deciding the total output of the economy, the society has to choose that combination of capital goods and consumer goods which is in keeping with its resources.

Problem 2: How to Produce these Goods?

The next basic problem of an economy is to decide about the techniques or methods to be used in order to produce the required goods. This problem is primarily dependent upon the availability of resources within the economy. If land is available in abundance, it may have extensive cultivation. If land is scarce, intensive methods of cultivation may be used. If labour is in abundance, it may use labour- intensive techniques; while in the case of labour shortage, capital-intensive techniques may be used.

The technique to be used also depends upon the type and quantity of goods to be produced. For producing capital goods and large outputs, complicated and expensive machines and techniques are required. On the other hand, simple consumer goods and small outputs require small and less expensive machines and comparatively simple techniques.

Further, it has to be decided what goods and services are to be produced in the public sector and what goods and services in the private sector. But in choosing between different methods of production, those methods should be adopted which bring about an efficient allocation of resources and increase the overall productivity in the economy.

Problem 3. For whom is the Goods Produced?

The third basic problem to be decided is the allocation of goods among the members of the society. The allocation of basic consumer goods or necessities and luxuries comforts and among the household takes place on the basis of among the distribution of national income. Whosoever possesses the means to buy the goods may have then. A rich person may have a large share of the luxuries goods, and a poor person may have more quantities of the basic consumer goods he needs.

Problem 4: How Efficiently are the Resources being Utilised?

This is one of the important basic problems of an economy because having made the three earlier decisions, the society has to see whether the resources it owns are being utilized fully or not. In case the resources of the economy are lying idle, it has to find out ways and means to utilize them fully.

Problem 5: Is the Economy Growing?

The last and the most important problem is to find out whether the economy is growing through time or is it stagnant. If the economy is stagnant at any point inside the production possibility curve, it has to be moved on to the production possibility curve PP whereby the economy now produces larger quantities of consumer goods and capital goods. Economic growth takes place through a higher rate of capital formation which consists of replacing existing capital goods with new and more productive ones by adopting more efficient production techniques or through innovations.

All of these economy problems will be our societies often causes to anyone feels need to solve problems in order to achieve our societies can have enough resources to satisfy our every day living.

● The Consumer Problem

Consumer theory is concerned with how a rational consumer would make consumption decisions. What makes this problem worthy of separate study, apart from the general problem of choice theory, is its particular structure that allows us to derive economically meaningful results. The structure arises because the consumer's choice sets are assumed to be defined by certain prices and the consumer's income or wealth. The consumer's problem is to choose that is most preferred or, equivalently, that has the greatest utility.

The assumption of perfect information is built deeply into the formulation of this choice problem, just as it is in the underlying choice theory. Some alternative models treat the consumer as rational but uncertain about the products, for example how a particular food will taste or a how well a cleaning product will perform. Some goods may be experience goods which the consumer can best learn about by trying ("experiencing") the good. In that case, the consumer might want to buy some now and decide later whether to buy more. That situation would need a different formulation. Similarly, if the agent thinks that high price goods are more likely to perform in a satisfactory way, that, too, would suggest quite a different formulation. Agents are price-takers. The agent takes prices p as known, fixed and exogenous. This assumption excludes things like searching for better prices or bargaining for a discount.

Hence , it seems that economic problems and consumer problems are similar, I feel that it is possible , economists can attempt to apply any economic theories to solve some consumer problems in some situations. They can find the accurate solutions when they can apply the suitable economic theories to solve the suitable consumer or economic problems in our societies. I shall indicate that how economists can apply the suitable economic theories to attempt to solve some consumer problems in our societies as below:

Demand And Supply Theory Solves Consumer Problems

What is economy rule predict consumer behaviour? Why and How does economist can apply economy rule to predict consumer behaviours? I shall explain the reasons as below:

Why does economic principle be the best to predict consumer behaviour. It may include these two reasons: The first focuses on the substantive domain of study, in this interpretation , economics is a social science devoted to understanding how the economy works. The second definition focuses on methods: economics is a way of doing social science, using particular tools. In this interpretation the discipline is associated with formal modelling and statistical analysis rather than particular hypotheses or theories about the economy. Therefore, economic methods can be applied to many other areas besides the economy, everything from decisions within the family to questions about political institutions.

● Demand and supply principle predict public transport tool passenger behaviour

Economists need to use the right economic ideas to predict consumer behaviour. So, Misuse the wrong economy ideas to predict consumer behaviours. It will do more wrong judgement to evaluate or predict why and how and when the country's consumer behaviours will change. It is every economist needs to consider issue. For example, the economy idea application of economic supply-demand principles to public transport. Different fares would give commuters with more-flexible hours the incentive to avoid peak travel times. They would allow passenger traffic to spread out over time, reducing the pressure on the public transport system when enabling even larger total passenger flow. IT aims to reduce traffic congestion, increased public-transport use, reduced car-bon emissions and cause air pollution and generated considerable revenue for the country's transport system. So, if the country can apply supply and demand economic principle to attempt to predict how many passengers number needs to catch transport tools to go to work or go to school or other activities. Then, it can predict how many bus, ferry, taxi, train, underground train, tram etc. different public transport tools to satisfy future public transport passengers' needs in society. So, this demand and supply principle is the comparative best rule to predict any kinds of public transport passengers' road needs, when they need to either go to school, go to office, go to leisure or shopping etc. different kinds of activities. So, applying the demand and supply principle to predict road and sea public transport passengers can help the country to reduce air pollution when they feel that they can find any public transport tools to catch any time conveniently , then it can encourage them to reduce car purchase desire. When many people choose to catch public transport tools, then it will reduce many cars number on the road. Then, air pollution will reduce as well as any public transport tools' income will also increase as well as traffic jam will also reduce. When the country can evaluate how many people choose to catch bus or taxi or ferry or train or underground train, or tram or train etc. different kinds of public transport tools, then the country can predict the more accurate public transport tools number to every kind of public transport tool to satisfy their journey needs. e.g. whether underground train or train or tram need to decrease or increase the frequent times or number to catch the volume of passenger in busy or non-busy time; or whether bus company has need to increase how much buses to catch the city location passengers when they are living in the city. Moreover, supply and demand principle can help any public transport tools to explain why their passengers number reduces in the year, it may due to fare charge is unreasonable, feeling uncomfortable to sit on the seat or air condition is poor in the transport tool environment, or there are no more seats because many there are much time is full passenger and no seat vacancy to provide to them to sit . So, supply and demand principle can help any kinds of public transport tools to find whether which is (are) the factor(S) can influence the current or last year passengers number reduce. Then, they can concentrate on improving their weaknesses to raise their service quality . So, supply and demand principle can also help they to evaluate whether what their weakness are in order to improve to increase passengers number. They can do questionnaires to enquiry their passengers' response to evaluate whether which areas of services that they feel unsatisfactory. So, the different kinds of service satisfactory feeling to the passengers number data will be the main source to help the kind of public transport tool to analyse and conclude the results more accurate, then they can make the more accurate judgement to improve the of service. For example, the questionnaires indicate that the many passengers feel the bus fare is reasonable, but many passengers feel they can not find any seats to sit easily. So, it implies that the bus firm ought buy more buses or enlarges bus size and increases more seats in the enlarged buses. Then, it does not reduce its fare but it needs to find solutions to let passengers can find seats to sit in every bus more easily. But, if the questionnaires indicate that there are many passengers feel its fare is higher or unreasonable to compare other kinds of public transportation tools. Hence, it can avoid to spend more expenditure to increase bus number to the city, if the city has many passengers , they still choose bus to catch, but they feel its fare is too higher to compare other kinds of public transport tool. Then, it only needs to reduce its fare , it ought help it to increase passengers number. Hence, demand and supply principle is the most suitable economic method to evaluate any kinds of public transport system passenger needs in any country nowadays.

● Supply and demand and price elasticities principle predict oil energy user behaviour

The another case is that demand and supply principle can predict oil buyer behaviour to find whether what factors can cause the oil buyer individual need reduces. For example , a rise in production costs increases market prices and reduces quantities demanded and supplied. Or when, energy cost rise, utility bills increases and households fid extra ways of saving heating and electricity. But, others are nor. For example, whether a tax is imposed on the producers or consumer of a commodity, say oil has nothing to do with who ends up paying for it. The tax might be administered on oil companies, but it might be consumers who really pay for it through higher prices at the pump. Or the extra cost might be imposed on consumers in the form of a sale tax, but the oil companies might be forces to absorb it through lower prices. It all depends on the " price elasticities" of demand and supply. With the addition of extra assumption, this model also generates rather strong implications about how well markets work. In particular, a competitive market economy is efficient in the sense that it is impossible to improve one person's well-being without reducing somebody.

● Demand and supply principle can misuse to predict consumer behaviour when the two firms participate advertisement to promote their products in the same time

Why can demand and supply principle misuse to predict consumer behaviour when the two firms participate advertisement to promote their products in the same time ? I shall explain as below: Assume that two competing firms must decide whether to have a big advertising budget. Advertising would allow one firm to steal some of the other's customers.

But when they both advertise, the effects on customer demand cancel out. The firms end up having spent money needlessly.

We might expect that neither firm would choose to spend much on advertising, but the model shows that this logic is off base. When the firms make their choices independently and they care only about their own profits, each one has an incentive to advertise, regardless of what the other firm does. When the other firm does not advertise, you can steal customers from it if you do advertise, when the other firm does advertise, you have to advertise to prevent loss of customers. So, these two firms end up in a bad equilibrium in which both have to waste resources. This market can not apply demand and supply principle to predict consumer behaviours because they depends advertisement to promote their products. If these two firms advertise their products in the same time. Then , it is not possible that if one firm increases it price and it will cause its customer number loss, due to its advertise can help it to attract customers to consider its product from television or radio or newspapers or magazine promotion channels. So, I suppose that these two firms decide to increase their price, when they advertise their products to let customers to know in the same time. They will not lose their customers or reduce their customers easily. Because their customers can be persuaded to choose to buy their products to compare other similar products in preference. So, their increasing price will not influence their customers number lose easily. It explains that demand and supply principle is not right to this case, so demand and supply principle can misuse to help them to predict consumer behaviours when they advertise their products in the same time. Also, demand and supply principle is not suitable to them to predict consumer behaviours when they advertise their products in the same time. They will do wrong prediction to their consumers purchase desire when they advertise their products in the same time.

ON conclusion, using these demand and supply and price elasticity techniques, economists derive specific prediction for how consumers choose which products to buy, how households save, how firms invest, how workers search for jobs, as well as for how these actions depend on the particulars. They can help them to predict job and consumption behaviours more accurate, it depends on whether the situation is right, such as both competition firms participate to advertise their products in the same time case, it is not right to apply above economic principle to predict consumer behaviours. They will get wrong prediction when they apply this principle

to predict consumer behaviours.
However, demand and supply principle can predict below any one of these cases. I shall indicate as below:
The problem of need-based scholarships: Most systems for providing college scholarships are based on some definition of financial needs, with scholarships generally being given only to those students who must need financial help in order to attend school.
Is need, rather than academic ability, the best basic on which to choose those students who are to be encouraged to attend college? Which way of choosing who gets aids is the more just? Which is the more efficient ? Is the overall educational level of society increased more by giving financial aid to bright students or to needy students? Presumably the aid offers more leverage to needy students, since they all need the money in order to attend college, whereas, many of the bright students would attend college in any case. But is a smaller number of bright students the more important addition?
So, the school can apply demand and supply principle to predict whether how many parents feel need financial assistance and evaluate how much financial amount is the right to borrow. It aims to calculate how many parents feel real financial need and how much to lend to them in order to let these students to get the most fair financial assistance.
Assuming the school wish to use need as a basis, how does the school determines " financial need"?
Is need a function or parents' income? What, then , does the school about children of wealthy parents who are living independently of them and get no aid from parents? Should they be punished for their parents' wealth? But if they are given aid, won't all students, in order to get aid, claim to be independent of their parents?

Is need solely a matter of family income, or should not the school takes a family's financial obligations into account? Does not it make more sense to give aid to someone whose parents must put night more children through school than to someone from a family of five or one only with the same income? But in a possible parallel situations, should a family that carries mortgages on one or two large homes get preference simply because they do not have much money left to spend on college? Does doing this reward ? Is there a difference between the case of night children and the case of the large mortgage? How should parents who are not married , but are living together and supporting their children jointly be counted? Most parents are

supporter to their children , although they are married in possible.
So, the school needs to gather all these data to evaluate how many parents are not married or married or living with their children together, how much salary they earn as well as every family has how much children as well as whether they have mortgage for their houses. So, these number will be the financial education assistance demanders, but it does not represent their real financial needs. It is possible that someone does not feel any financial need, although their children apply financial assistance to your school. Then , your school needs to evaluate whether how much financial assistance can lend to every real financial need student family. It can not exceed your final financial expenditure budget (supply) , when your financial expenditure is not enough. SO, demand and supply principle can be applied to research this school real family financial demand to lend to the real financial need families and evaluate whether the reasonable financial amount to lend to every child family to study in your school.

● Supply and demand principle applies to immigration to decide wage case

A fascinating and important example of supply and demand, full of complexities, is the role of immigration in determining wages. If you ask people , they are likely to tell you that immigration into California or Florida US, surely lowers the wages of people in those regions. It is just supply and demand analysis of immigration. According to this analysis, of these to these two regions in US. Immigration in to a region shifts the supply curve for labor to the right and pushes down wages. Why has it relationship between immigration to US these two regions immigrant number and wage?

Careful economic studies cast doubt on this simple proposition, however, a recent survey of the evidence concludes:

The effect of immigration on the labor market outcomes of natives is small in US. There is no evidence of economically significant reductions in native employment. Most analysis, finds that a 10 percent increase in the fraction of immigrants in the population reduced native wages by a most 1%.

How can we explain the small impact of immigration on wages? The main mistake is to forget how mobile the American population is and that the impact of immigration on wages, we must examine the effect of new immigrants when the strength of the local economy and the number of native-born residents in a city are unchanged, that is , when these other things are held constant. Unless you exclude the effects other changing variables, you can not accurately predict the impact of immigration. The same principle holds in doing a supply0and demand analysis of any market. As much as possible, when you are examining the impact of a supply or demand shift, you must try to keep all other things constant.

- Rationing by prices

By determining the equilibrium prices and quantities of all inputs and outputs, the market allocated or rations out the scare goods of the society among the possible uses. Who does the rationing? A planning board? Congress or the president? BO, the marketplace, through the interaction of supply and demand, doe the rationing. This is rationing by the purse.

What foods are produces? This is answered by the signals of the market price. High oil prices stimulates oil production, whereas low food prices drive resources out of agriculture. Those who have the most dollars votes have the greatest influences on what goods are produced. All of these considers how demand and supply to the market.

For whom are goods produces? The power of the pursue indicates the distribution of income and consumption. Those with higher incomes end up with larger houses, more clothing, and linger vacations. When the most urgently felt needs get fulfilled through the demand curve.

Even, the how question is decided by supply and demand. When corn prices are low, it is not profitable for farmers to use expensive tractors and irrigation systems, and only the best land is cultivated. When oil prices are high, oil companies drill in deep offshore waters and employ novel seismic techniques to find oil.

IN sum , any thing needs through demands, interact with costs of goods, as reflected in supplies in our economic world. Hence, demand and supply theory ought be the most accurate method to help any businesses or governments to predict their shareholders behaviours when they will change as well as how and how their behaviours change.

CHAPTER TWO

Consumer choice theory solves consumer problems

What is 'consumer choice theory'?

'Consumer choice theory' is a hypothesis about why people buy things. Put simply, it says that you choose to buy the things that give you the greatest satisfaction, while keeping within your budget. At the heart of this theory are three assumptions about human nature.[1]

The first assumption is that when you shop, you choose to buy things based on calculated decisions about what will make you happiest. In economics language, this is known as utility maximisation (Economists really like to put quite simple concepts into long complicated terms.)

Secondly, the theory assumes that no matter how much you shop, you will never be completely satisfied. In other words, you will always be happier consuming a little bit more. This is known as the principle of non-satiation.

Thirdly, even though you always get more happiness from more consumption, the amount of pleasure you get from each good decreases with the more you consume. So if you eat two ice creams rather than one, you get more overall pleasure, but the second ice-cream won't be as satisfying as the first. This is known as decreasing marginal utility.

Consumer choice theory has influenced everything from government policy to corporate advertising to academia. But the theory has been criticized for not being the most accurate description of how people actually make choices. A whole new branch of economics, called 'behavioral economics', has emerged essentially to use findings from psychology to disprove the assumptions behind consumer choice theory. This has also led others to argue that consumer choice theory is less about describing how we do actually behave, and is more about describing how people should behave.[3] In other words, by portraying people as self-interested shopaholics, economists are saying that is it okay and natural for us to be avid consumers.

● Consumer choice theory can be applied to solve consumer problems during the country can have economic growth , the reasons may include as below:

The scenario leading to inflation starts with poor growth. Forget about everything that comes next and focus on that most important factor. Because it happens that the scenario leading to a budget crisis also starts with poor growth, and the scenario leading to a long-term unemployment crisis starts with poor growth, and a scenario leading to a better-the-neighbor trade crisis starts with poor growth, and so on. So a very important question is: what can be done to improve the prospects for economic growth? In particular, what is the right countercyclical approach to take to best situate the economy for future growth? I shall indicate during US, America's economy growth occurs, then economists can attempt to apply customer choice theory to solve US itself country's consumer problems more easier.

In no small part, the question comes down to interpretations of charts like the one at right. On the one hand, long and deep downturns seem to have almost no effect on the long-term rate of growth. On the other hand, in the long run we're all dead, and those who live during an extended period of economic weakness suffer for it. Meanwhile, it's also difficult to see where high debt levels influence the long-run rate of growth, at least where this chart is concerned.

During to the medium-term growth stage, is the bigger threat to American growth rates a market revolt against American debt levels? Or is it structural unemployment stemming from the slow, jobless recovery? Or is the cyclical shortfall in public investment? Or something else entirely? Of course, there's no real reason one has to choose a problem to address at the expense of others. More aggressive monetary expansion could make the finding of a solution to all these problems easier, but the Fed is unwilling to oblige me on this score. It may well be concerned that lack of fiscal discipline will lead to increasing inflation expectations, making its job harder (but then fiscal problems are trace able to growth). If that is the worry, however, one has to ask why the Congress has been unable to strike a deal for $20 billion in stimulus this year for $80 billion in fiscal tightening in a year or two (fill in whatever amounts you wish). But the outlook for the American economy vis-a-vis any number of potential crises will hinge on growth, and growth will hinge on the ability of private business to exploit promising opportunities as they arise. And the question is: what's likely to hurt that ability most? High interest rates? Lack of consumer demand? A shortage of adequately prepared workers? Right now firms appear to be most worried about demand shortfalls. So how much can you boost demand without making the primary fear high interest rates? A lot, if the expansion is on the monetary side.

● How to supply consumer choice theory to predict Consumer Behavior Marketing at Apple Computer

During US economy growth, Apply computer applies consumer choice theory to solve its computer buyers' choice problems among different kinds of brand computer competitors. Have you ever wondered why Apple is so successful? They were not the first company to invent the personal computer, portable music device, the tablet, the smartphone, software to download music, or the set-top box to name a few. Apple has amassed a brand loyal following like no other brand backed by significant sales, market share, and profitability. So, how does Apple do it? What's the secret behind their success?

Marketing using consumer behavior insight is how Apple succeeds. Even though Steve Jobs and Apple, did not use consumer research in the initial development of most products, consumer behavior plays a huge role in their marketing and ultimately the success of the company. Once a consumer purchases a product or downloads iTunes Apple has access to data the company leverages. Apple uses this information to gain significant insight into the consumer and what drives purchase behavior.

Consumer behavior marketing is an essential ingredient in the current business climate. The companies that apply this type of marketing well have a distinct competitive advantage that distances them from their rivals. Consumer behavior research is the primary driver at the core of any good strategy. Research provides actionable insight and ensures business success. If you answer no to the following questions, this post is for you?

•Are you applying consumer behavior marketing currently?

•Have you conducted consumer behavior research within the last two years?

•Do you have consumer behavior marketing in your marketing plan with well-defined marketing strategies and tactics?

•Are you achieving the maximum results for your organization?

Every business has a target audience and consumer behavior marketing

provides the fundamental methods for understanding your target. Consumer behavior research provides the underlying element that drives quality strategies and ensures business results.
"Marketing is understanding your buyers really, really well. Then creating valuable products, services, and information especially for them to help solve their problems."
The organizations that have an intimate understanding of their target audience possess a competitive advantage over those that do not. Establishing a one-to-one relationship and thorough knowledge of your target audience is a core responsibility for business in the 21st century and beyond. Regardless if you are B2B, B2C, B2G or a hybrid organization you have a target audience. The information in this post can be applied to any business type. This post focuses on Apple (B2C) employing consumer behavior marketing as a critical ingredient for their success.
Hence, Apply computer shops have several computer teachers to teach any visitors how to use its laptops, hen they enquire its any computer salespeople. Due to its salespeople had been trained to learn how to use the different kinds of laptops. So, anyone enquires them, they can answer their enquires concern any computer questions immediately. Then, they will feel Apple laptops are the first choice to compare other kinds of laptops brands. It is one salespeople answering strategies to persuade any Apple computer visitors to feel its any laptops are the first or preference choice to compare its competitors in this computer market, so customer choice economic theory is the most suitable strategy to solve Apple computer's customer individual purchase decision problem.

Microeconomics Models and Theories solve customer problems

Microeconomics is concerned with the economic decisions and actions of individuals and firms. Within the broad church of microeconomics, there are different theories that certain assumptions and expectations of economic behaviour. The most important theory is neo-classical theory, which places emphasis on free-markets and the assumption individuals are rational and seek to maximise utility. However, there are many critiques of the neo-classical model, arguing economics is more complex with issues of market failure and irrational behaviour.

Pre-classical microeconomic theory

Before, Adam Smith, economics was more disparate with no commanding overall theory. Philosophers like Aristotle and Plato made references to issues in economics such as division of labour. The dominant ideas, pre-classical economics, were based on theories of mercantilism – the idea a nation should try to accumulate gold.

Classical microeconomic theory

Classical microeconomic theory was developed by Adam Smith (Wealth of Nations, 1776) and later economists, such as David Ricardo The essential aspect of classical microeconomic theory include:

Adam Smith mentioned the 'invisible hand of the market.' He noted how when people act out of self-interest, markets tend to provide goods and services which are demanded by the population. It needed no central price setting, but market forces responded to changes in demand and supply, e.g. a shortage pushes up the price and causes demand to fall.

Smith also investigated topics such as the division of labour, specialisation and economies of scale. The early classical economists emphasised the importance of costs to firms and consumers.

Utility maximisation

An important development of classical economics towards the end of the nineteenth century is the concept of utility maximisation. The concept of utility was developed by philosophers/economists – Jeremy Bentham and John Stuart Mill. In microeconomic theory, it was believed a consumer will buy goods depending on the marginal utility (satisfaction) they get from the good. This theory assumes consumers are rational and seeking to maximise the satisfaction they get.

Neo-classical theory

Neo-classical theory is a modern re-interpretation of classical economics of the nineteenth century. Neo-classical theory places importance on markets, but developed new ideas, especially regarding utility and rational choice theory. Elements of neo-classical theory.

1. Market distribution of goods and services.
2.R ational choice theory. This is the idea individuals hold rational preferences and make rational choices; seeking to maximise their outcomes – be it profit, wages, consumption or investment.
3. People act independently and make use of available information.
4. Marginalism. In neo-classical economics, more emphasis was placed on concepts of marginal utility and marginal cost. We make choices depending on satisfaction we get from one extra unit of a good.

Economists such as Carl Menger, William Stanley Jevons and Marie-Esprit-Léon Walras. and Alfred Marshall developed ideas such as diminishing marginal utility. Many of these neo-classical economic theories were brought together in Alfred Marshall's very influential textbook, Principles of Economics. (1890)

•Note there is some blurring between classical economics and neo-classical economics.

•Neo-classical economics has also come to mean 'orthodox economic theory. To a large extent, it has incorporated new developments in microeconomics, such as theories of market failure, market structure and econometrics.

Theories of Market failure

Neo-classical economics has become associated with a belief in the efficiency of markets. However, microeconomic theory has also incorporated the criticisms and limitations of free-markets.

•Monopoly. Adam Smith was well aware of the problem of monopolies and how firms could use their market power to set excessive prices.

•Imperfect competition. In the 1930s, Joan Robinson developed a model of imperfect competition, an awareness many markets were somewhere between monopoly and perfect competition often assumed in neo-classical economics.

•Externalities. Developed by Arthur C.Pigou in The Economics of Welfare (1920) this is the awareness production and consumption decisions can have harmful (or positive) effects on third parties. Therefore, a free market can lead to overconsumption of demerit goods and negative externalities.

•Game theory. An awareness, decisions are not linear or simple, but the interdependence of agents influences what we decide to do.

Behavioural economics

The most important trend in recent decades in economics is the greater emphasis placed on aspects of behavioural economics, which uses many insights from related fields such as psychology.

•Disputes rational choice theory. The essential element of behavioural economics is that it argues individual agents are often not rational and often do not seek to maximise utility.

•Behavioural economics examines how agents can be influenced by biases, and make decisions not predicted by neo-classical economic theory. Behavioural economics can explain the irrational exuberance of booms and busts.

Econometrics

In the post-war period, economics became increasingly mathematical with economists attempting to use mathematics to explain models and theories. Econometrics looks at economic data and seeks to extract simple relationships. The basic tool is the linear regression models and can be used to try and predict consumer spending and demand for labour.

Heterodox models of microeconomics

Heterodox models differ substantially from microeconomic foundations of neo-classical economics. Schools of thought include

Marxist economic theory

Karl Marx developed an alternative perspective on economics. He focused on the surplus value created under the capitalist economic system. To Marx, the invisible hand of the market would be better described as the invisible hand of capitalist exploitation of workers. Marx claimed workers did receive their full labour value but were compensated for their necessary labour only – enabling capitalists to profit from the surplus.

Institutional economics. The role of society and institutions in shaping economic behaviour. For example, Thomas Veblen looked at theories of 'conspicuous consumption' and noted how the desire for social status could drive much economic theory. Institutional economics could be seen as a forerunner for later behavioural economics.

Environmental economics Argues traditional economics wrongly places value on increasing output. The most important thing is creating a sustainable environment which maximises living standards. So, manufacturers need to consider how to manufacture their products , but pollution can not be raised as the same time, because human will face to raise cost of living and living experiences to be poor , even food shortage, water pollution , air pollution , death rate raises when technological productivities brings pollution to our natural environment. Hence, environmental economoic theory is the most suitable to solve manufacturers' pollution problem.

Buddhist economics/non-profit goals. Like environmental economics, this questions the assumption higher incomes and higher output are desirable. The theory of hedonistic relativism suggests higher incomes do nothing to increase happiness levels, and traditional economics can encourage society to pursue materialistic goals which actually create more problems of stress, conflict and environmental degradation.

Some of the basic models you might find in A-Level economics :

•Price Discrimination

•Perfect competition
•Price Mechanism
•Monopoly
•Oligopoly and kinked demand curve
•Game Theory Pricing strategies
•Market failure
•Behavioural economics

ON conclusion, any macro economy theories can be applied to find the most reasonable methods to solve any customer problems in societies by economists as above. So, I believe that any economic and customer and social problems can be solved by economic theories in our society.

CHAPTER THREE

E-service quality innovation successful factor

Nowadays, many businesses are international trading, due to globalization and opening of markets. E-commerce will be the most popular advertisement and sale method to help any kinds of businesses to promote products to let many clients to know effectively in short time. However, e-ecommerce will bring new organizational structure change to help any organizations to improve performance management, organizational development, and continuous and cumulative process of improvement of multi-national companies, when the organization can have e-commerce sale strategy. I believe that the e-commerce sale strategy can help any organizations to raise sale growth more easily. I shall explain the reasons as below:

On innovation and e-service quality for developing e-retailing mass entrepreneurship aspect, it can bring rapid sale growth advantage to the e-commerce organization, it also needs the business leader has clear vision to create and maintain his learning organization, such as the e-commerce learning organization, e.g. Amazon is a successful e-learning, e-commerce learning organization. It is a e-retailing middleman to help any businesses to sell and delivery their products to clients' homes. When any clients click Amazon website, they can find any kinds of products, e.g. travel bags, computers, books and magazines, movie and music CD, DCD, home, electronic and health etc. products. So, after they paid visa to buy its any its any kinds of products from its website. Then, Amazon will deliver these products to their homes within one week. It can provide rapid product delivery service to let them to feel sale and after sale service satisfactory feeling. Hence, Amazon is a good example of continuous learning in its organizational life, a process helps self understanding, self management and self actualization e-commerce organization. However, Amazon' successful factors can concern on innovation and delivery efficient service, skillful online sale and online management skills are its main successful factors. Moreover, Amazon can apply psychological knowledge to assist workers to raise industrialized efficiency . It can s managers ought know how help every worker to create talent ability and co-operate to work efficiently in teams during innovation process.

In fact, product technique innovation will be another factor to raise any businesses' competitive effort, e.g. reducing cost benefit aim. So, when the organization can raise new productive technique to help them to reduce manufacturing cost. Then, it will reduce finance burden to the organization for long time. Hence, learning low cost e-service
technique will be one main factor to stable any organizations' existence or alive in long time.

IN business environment, since internet is popular, it can influence customers shopping method to be changed to online purchase channel. So, e-commerce can replace traditional walk-in store purchase channel. Online purchase can bring these benefits to consumers, such as rapid product information search, visa card payment method, safe and quiet home environment purchasing activities, free product delivery and return or refund after sale service conveniently. Moreover, e-commerce or e-retailing business can bring more business activities with more economic growth and supporting technological manufacturing development.

How to attract or encourage consumers' online shopping consumption desires? It is one very important view point, because when one consumer has online shopping desire, then he will have online shopping or buying activity to find the e-retailer's website to click from its website in possible. So, any e-retailers must need to excite their potential online consumers have e-platforms click in their websites to search products desires or needs in preference more than walk in stores to search products method on street. However, I believe that their online product photos whether are attractive or their wirelesses are high or rapid mobile linking speed will influence their online businesses in success. So, online e-service and wireless rapid speed performances will influence every online retailer individual success or fail, instead of product photos whether are clear or information search whether is rapid or enough and sale price whether is low or reasonable and after sale support performance whether is satisfactory factors. So, e-service quality, e-platform, e-product photo and search information performance

these will be main factor to influence whether the e-retailer's sale growth. For example, Amazon book company is one famous and successful online e-book publisher among of the similar online e-book publishers, instead of itself e-middleman product delivery service provision to global buyers. It's success is due to its e-technology is often innovated in product delivery service, such as it has both efficiency after sale service and product delivery departments, of rapid delivery products to any countries' buyers within several days only, e-mail or phone feedback
to every e-buyer's enquiry, such as it organizes different kinds of enquiry questions to let its indicated staffs to answer the kind of indicated enquiry question only. So, its enquiring department staffs can avoid to spend much time to find answers to solve any enquires. In management view, it is " division of labours" concept to be used in Amazon customer service department. Also, it has large warehouse, it applied robotics to help warehouses to find and delivery any kinds of products to the correct delivery positions in order to delivery the product to the client's destination in the short time. So, robotics had help Amazon to reduce warehouse staffs' times and raises efficiencies in warehouses. When the warehouse workers can receive the client name and address and product kind and product purchase number data from its Amazon website e-retail store channel. Then, its warehouse staffs can follow these data to let robotics to know where they need to arrive to find the product(s) and deliver them to the right positions and let the lorry drivers to deliver to either airport (overseas buyers) or local destination (home country buyers). So, e-service quality performance will influence Amazon's product delivery or after sale service performance.

What does e-commerce bring positive or negative impact to traditional publish industry? it seems that e-commerce has an important influence to impact traditional book shop publish industry. Nowadays, due to many publishers begin to choose to apply e-platform to help any publishers themselves to sell their books either e-book format or paper book format. SO, many readers can read e-books from e-book shop or book shops do not need authors to print lot of paper books to put in warehouses before. Because any book shops can apply their e-book store to let readers to choose any topic books from their e-publishing stores , then they can pay visa either to read e-book from their e-book platform or e-library or print the number paper books to be delivered to their homes. So, publishers do not need to print many books for every author before none any readers pay to

buy their books from walk-in book stores. It means that the publisher do not need any traditional walk-in book shops to let them to visit, because the reader can click to the publisher's e-platform and he find any book information to chose which book(s) , he want to buy. He can pay visa to choose either read e-book from its e-platform or e-library or print on demand. So, the warehouse won't have excess book stocks to be kept in warehouses often and the printing costs will decrease as well as
none any old books to need to reduce price to sell because there has none any books stores to be kept in warehouses. So, it can bring waste warehouse places and waste paper printing economic and reducing sale price economic benefits to the e-publisher and readers both, such as Amazon publisher is using this e-service performance method.

E-commerce had changed the young age and female and male sex consumers shopping attitude. Bigne, Enrique (2005) indicated that the main users of online shopping were young men with a high level of income and a university education. This profile is changing. For example, in USA in the early years of internet where were very few women users, but by 2001 year, women were 52.8% of the online population . Socio-cultural pressure has made men generally more independent in their purchase decisions, when women place greater value on personal contact and social relations.
What is the main factor to bring some e-retailers' success. I believe that how to innovate e-service quality, which will be the main successful factor. The reasons may include as below:

There are too many e-retailers sell their products in this e-platform market. So, competition is serious. If one e-retailer could innovate its e-service performance, then its e-service quality will let its online visitors to fell its e-platform or e-store is more unique to compare its similar competitors. It will bring more attractive to raise its competitive ability.

Falk(2005) explained gave these useful opinions for your reference. They may include: The main idea of online shopping is not in having a good looking website that could be listed in a lot of search engines and it is not about the act behind the site ; it also is not only just not disseminating information, because it is all about building relationships and making money; mostly, organizations try to adopt techniques of online shopping without understanding these techniques and/or without a sound business model; rather than supporting the organization's culture and brand name, the website should satisfy customer's expectations; a majority of consumers choose online shopping for faster and more efficient shopping experience;

many researchers notify that the uniqueness of the web has dissolved and the need for the design, which will be user centered is very important; companies should always remember that there are certain things, such as understanding
the customer's wants and needs, living up to promises, never go out of style, because they give reason to come back. All of his opinions concern how to innovate the e-service quality
in order to atract many e-visitors to the e-retailer's website or e-platform or e-store more easily.

As Mc Donaldization theory can be used in terms of online shopping case, because online shopping and Mc Donald restaurant was becoming more popular. Such as Mc Donaldization is one global restaurant business, it has four major principles: efficiency, calculability, predictability and control. So they have similar views, any e-retailers‘ e-service quality need include: How to predict their e-visitors' online shopping desire absolutely, if they can raise their e-shopping desires, then their sale chance will increase; efficient wireless
speed, after e-sale service provision, efficient warehouse e-client data rapid receipt information for product rapid deliviery service arrangement and avoiding delivery error occurrence;
calculate e-visitor click in website times and controlling they desire to click their websites long time in order to increase shopping transaction occurrence chance and increase visa payment amount and the different kinds of products purchases number.

Why does e-service need to be innovated? Invitation can improve performance, raise productivity, increase yield and output and create growth as well as it can reduce waste, minimize
environment damages. Parasuraman, Zeithaml, and Berry (1988) showed that e-service quality is the strategy that is gaining momentum for online business operators to position themselves
more effectively in the marketplace. Because when any e-visitors click to any e-retailers‘ websites, they will compare any one e-retailer's website performance, if they feel comfortable
or better emotion to the e-retailer's website. Then, they will be attracted to choose to click the e-retailer's website one more time again, even more times. SO, how to let e-consumers
feel the e-retailer's website is unique or different to other general e-retailers' websites .(differentiates products or services, differentiation

comes from the e-retailer's website name, e.g. http://www.topicecream.com for the ice cream food, unique website design, packaging and delivery service use of wireless speed technology, unique features , e.g. attracting online shopping process, not complex or simple to research any products informatio from the e-retailer's website, extraordinary customer service, e.g. rapid customer enquiry feedback, take care after e-sale delivery service. All of these are important factors to cause any e-retailers' successes. Hence, it the e-retailer can have unique e-service provision to let any e-visitors to fee. Then, I believe that their product sale price can still keep higher and their customer number will not be influenced to reduce when they choose e-platform to sell their products.

Moreover, the e-retailing website managers need to build good learning insights to predict e-consumer behaviors. Such as consumers' living ways, life style, quality of life, service quality , inspiration, innovation, creativity, curiosity, design thinking, execution. Because when the e-retailer's website managers can have good analysis to judge whether what reasons or factors can influence his e-consumers choose to buy ot not buy his products after they click in whose website store. What reasons cause they change their traditional walk in shops shopping habits. So, how to persuade walk-in consumers to choose to click in the e-retailer's website store. If the e-retailer can persuade them to increase click in whose website times. Then, its online transaction will increase more easily. Hence, it has relationship between click in the e-retailer's website times and the e-service performance innovation.

● Building customer loyalty to online electronic manufacturing services e-commerce industry

Customer loyalty is critical to the success of an electronic manufacturing services. Internet invention can bring electronic manufacturing development. However, electronic manufacturing businessmen need to research these question in order to develop in success: What are the most common factors as well as the critical successful factors affect buyer loyalty ?

In fact, customer loyalty means to relate to consumer buying behaviors, such as electronic manufacturing service industry, if the electronic manufacturing service provider can provide satisfactory electronic manufacturing service to any consumers or it can build good global customer relationship from internet by website advertisement and e-mail communication both channels.

In technological aspect, such as rapid speed internet access, PC household penetration. Hence, when one online client can click the electronic manufacturing company website. Then, he can find many attractive electronic manufacturing product from the internet clear electronic manufacturing product photos. When, he can research any kinds of electronic manufacturing products from the company's website easily and he also feels the photos can show their characteristics or features , e.g. colour, size, price indicated. Then, he can understand every electronic manufacturing product clearly. So, the online bring successful chance will increase, even if the company can provide good enquiry service to him, when he sends email to enquire the individual customer service staff and he can answer his enquiry immediately by the company's email.

In general , because any electronic products are usually small size, to their photos must have large size to let any online visitors to see every electronic parts of every electronic product photo in the e-commerce company website. Every online visitor also needs to know every electronic manufacturing product from every photo, e.g. whether the electronic manufacturing product (laptop or desktop) has discount, how much discount percentage, e.g. 20% and original price and after discount price information from the company website. Hence, every electronic product photo needs to let any online visitors to know all of price information from itself company website clearly. If every can not indicate actual clear price information that will influence their buying decision to be delayed. So, buying transaction will not succeed easily. So, e-ecommerce on electronic manufacturing product industry , it will be more difficult to achieve transaction success from internet channel. If the company can not show its any electronic manufacturing products to let every online visitor to feel understanding clearly.

On conclusion, good quality technological factor will be important to influence electronic manufacturing products e-commerce in success. One repeat online ecommerce electronic manufacturing product buyer who must need to feel much understanding to every electronic product features and characteristics from every firm's website online photos, price issues when he see those photos from the company's website. So, the online electronic manufacturing product buyers' loyalty is built on technological service quality, on time delivery service , past satisfactory or dissatisfactory online search experience to the firm's website, technological and unique website attraction to the firm's website of E-service quality innovation successful factor will influence any e-retailer's success.

Reference

Bigne, Enrique (2005). The impact of internet user shopping patterns and demographics on consumer mobile buying.

Falk, Louis, K. et. al (2005) " E-commerce and consumer's expectations: What makes a website work". Journal of website promotion, 1(1), 65-75.

Parasuraman, A., Zeithaml, V.A. and Berry L.L. (1988) SERVQUAL: A multiple-item scale for measuring consumer perceptions of
service quality. Journal of retailing, 64, 12-40.

Globalization e-commerce
Development brings
China " one belt, one road
Strategy" advantages

Globalization can bring China " one belt, one road strategy" global social economic advantages, such as China's 21 St. century " one belt , one road strategy. It aims to bring the different Asia countries, even Western countries' business cooperation more easily after it had built high speed railway to go to different countries which had road transport to link to China on land. So, in long term benefits, China businessmen can cooperate to these participative "one belt, one road strategy businessmen to carry on buying and selling their unique products from road transport conveniently. Even, e-commerce can bring important economic advantages to influence this " one belt, one road strategy " in success. I shall explain the reasons that why e-commerce can bring business advantages to them as below:

China's "one belt, one road strategy " aims to achieve the global world share GNP 55% , as well as global consumer number of 77% and global energy saves 75%. Instead of existing trading investment, China also compromises to provide US one hundred billion dollar of basic facility fund, central Asia one belt, one road strategy fund of forty billion US dollar to invest this "one belt, one road strategy" of long term business development. I believe that it seems that China only hopes to build railway facility and encourage the participative countries to build factories to invest to do businesses between China and these countries as well as create jobs to solve China unemployment ratio, but in fact, I believe that China will apply e-commerce technology to assist its businessmen to do online trading more easily. I shall indicate the reasons to explain that why e-commerce and

China 's one belt, one road strategy , they have close economic growth of case and effect relationship.

China will be only one globalization main essential " one belt, one road strategy" country to control all participative countries' businessmen activities and China can help the excess of developing countries' economic development in the same tie. In fact, internet can assist China's future economic development. The reason is that I believe that when China's " one belt, one road strategy " can develop to succeed. It can encourage many " one belt, one road strategy" participative countries businessmen to be persuaded to apply internet technology to do e-commerce in the same time after the railway transport facilities are built to let all of these participative countries businessmen can transport their products to their cities from road transport more easily and rapidly. So, it can being short time product transport advantages when the participative country's consumers buy the product from the online platform as well as the product can be delivered to his home from railway transport rapidly. So, e-commerce and railway transport has close relationship to cause this business activities in success. For example, one Asia "one belt, one road strategy country's participative businessman , he can apply e-commerce technology to sell its products to Western countries , e.g. US, UK online clients in short time rapidly.

The participative countries may include India, Greece, Serbia, Hungary etc. 66 countries. So, these one belt, one road strategy participative countries can cooperate to do e-commerce business to sell themselves unique products to the non-participative "one belt, one road strategy" countries from e-commerce channel. When these non-participative " one belt, one road strategy " countries consumers have none of the kinds products to buy from themselves countries, but they click to these participative " one belt, one road strategy" countries participation businessmen themselves web stores to find the kinds of products which can buy from their web stores. Then, they can apply online to buy the products from these one belt, one road strategy countries' businessmen web stores more easily and conveniently in short time. The important factor is railway transport, when these products can be delivered from railway from China to these participative countries. For example, when one participative country businessman , he has none of this kind of product to sell to the US or US client, but he apply internet channel to click to the China businessman's web store to find the kind of product that he can sell. SO, he can apply internet channel to buy the Chins business's product after he pays visa.

The China e-retailer can deliver the kind of product to his store by railway transport rapidly. Railway transport can reduce the transport cost , when the e-retailer (buyer) does not need to pays air freight fee. It is more cheap transport cost. Then, the participative " one belt, one road strategy " e-retailer can deliver the kind of product to the US, or UK buyer by air transport rapidly when he find the kind of product which can be provided from the China e-retailer from online channel immediately. So, railway building and e-commerce channel will influence the " one belt, one road strategy " in success.

The 21 St century sea transport considers different countries consumers' buying need when they feel that they can not buy the kinds of products from themselves countries easily. So, such as the participative " one belt, one road strategy" countries , they can transport their products between China and themselves countries by railway transport, then the sea transport will not be popular to help them to deliver their products because sea transport delivery speed must be slower than railway transport. Any consumers won't hope to receive their products in long transport time. So, railway transport must be one important transport factor to influence China 's "one belt, one road strategy" in success.

Moreover, e-commerce invention can help these participative " one belt, one road strategy" countries e-retailers to apply web stores sale channel to cooperate to sell their unique products between them. When one country e-retailer can buy the another country retailer 's product from web store and it can be delivered to its country by railway transport , then it can still supply the kind of product to the e-consumer , even it has non any of this kind of product stock in its warehouse. Railway transport can help them to deliver their products from road in short time between China and these participative countries. So, they must have geographic advantage to deliver their products rapidly after railway transport facilities are built successfully between China and these countries. Moreover, web store can help them to advertise their products to let the non-participative "one belt, one road strategy" countries consumers to know whether which kinds of products these participative countries e-retailers , they can sell from themselves web stores when they click to their websites to see their product photos immediately.

So, China's " one belt, one road strategy" can influence to achieve global online ecommerce advantage for China and the participative " one belt, one road strategy 66 countries e-retailers and e-commerce can help them to promote their any products to Western countries to let they to know in short time rapidly.

ON currency gain benefit aspect, in fact, e-commerce can help this " one belt, one road strategy" participative countries earn exchange rate transaction more easily because when the non-participative " one belt, one road strategy " countries consumers pay visa to buy their products from their web stores. Usually, they need to pay US dollar to buy their products by visa card for every online transaction. So, when these participative "one belt, one road strategy" online e-retailers receive their US payment by visa. They have more currency earn chance when US dollar needs to exchange high local exchange to their dollar. So, the currency exchange earn will have possible to occur from e-commerce. For example, when one e-US consumer buys one product from the China's online e-retailer , when the e-US consumer pays US currency to buy it by visa. Then, the China E-RETAILER can receive the US currency sale profit and change to Chinese dollar to earn the foreign exchange income when it find decides to change the US currency to Chinese currency in the right time.

So, e-commerce globalization can also raise foreign exchange earn chance between the countries' online consumers and the another e-retailers when they are carrying any e-commerce activities. Hence, e-commerce can assist the China's " one belt, one road strategy" development more success between Asia and Western countries.

However, the internet development can help China's 21 St century " one belt, one road strategy" to achieve these aspects of development, instead of e-commerce development. The five major achievements are such as , 1. Policy coordination, 2. Facilities connectivity, 3. Going out trade, 4. Financial integration, increased economic performance and productivity and 5. Encouraging people to people e-commerce transaction. Because internet development can help any countries consumers to search new products information as well as helping them to cooperate to analyze and achieving the best effective and efficient online shopping activities. So, it may reduce the incentives and opportunities for terrorist movement. Such as Beijing is becoming a top salesman city to promote the China made products and in big discount with some conditions when to achieve the global of made in China e-commerce in " one belt, one road strategy" 2025.

ON conclusion, internet invention can help China and the 66 participative one belt, one road strategy" countries to gather any new products information as well as discusses how they can operate do this global e-commerce in success. Nowadays, the world is focus on the China movement on the one belt, one road strategy, how impact of the international financial crisis keeps rapidly, the world economy is recovering slowly, and global development is uneven. So, internet development can encourage the international trade and investment for the participative one belt and one road strategy countries and even these countries still facing big challenges to their e-commerce development. So, internet can assist the one belt, one road strategy cooperative countries' information exchange to achieve success. Internet can help them to bring an economic area through building infrastructure, increasing culture exchange and broadening global e-commerce development. This innovative conceptual strategy will bring China to take a bigger role in global affairs and it is an easy way to let China to export China's reserve products in area of " over production" , such as electrical appliances, steel aluminum , railway equipment and building's material manufacturing between China and the participative countries by railway transport. Internet can help it to apply e-commerce channel to promote its material products to let overseas buyers to know from their web stores in short time. So, internet can bring successful advertisement promotion development to China and the 66 participative one belt, one road countries on overseas online e-commerce sale chance absolutely. Finally, internet can also bring further deepening and expanding beneficial cooperation in such areas as trade, investment, finance, transport and communication aspects to these participative one belt, one road strategy countries. For China example, it is the world's largest producer of gold and also major importer and consumer. It can apply e-commerce trading method to promote its gold products to global gold buyers from the gold sellers' web stores in short time. When the country's one gold buyer research the China's one gold online retailer web store to find its quality and appearance is more attractive to compare his country gold shops. Then, he will pay visa to buy the China gold e-retailer's gold from its web store by visa immediately. So, e-commerce can help China's gold e-retailers to promote their gold products to let global gold buyers to know from their web stores in the short time. Hence, global e-commerce activity can help China to promote products and increase sale chance in short time after its one, belt, one road strategy can implement to achieve successfully.

CHAPTER FOUR

Behavioral Economic Theory

Socio-economic means that investigators had been addressing the key issues of mental life: Thinking, problem solving, the nature of consciousness. Their concept of human nature, human decision making in psychology. Economists understood utility in terms of conscious experience like pleasure or happiness. Utility arises from any commodity must be considered as measured by happiness. The some suitable quantitative measure of utility, or satisfaction, or desiredness.

However, economists research these questions concern consumer, such as : questions of motivation, preference formation and choice. In psychological view,human judgement and decision making and behavioral economics have always been concerned about psychological as well as sociological and variables as determinants of choice, which together , lend themselves to a better understanding choice behavior of consumption and production. The key points, critical to behavioral economics may indicate:

Assumptions are caused by causal and predictive analysis, be they of a psychological, sociological. It is important to understand why people behave the way they do, a critical component of behavioral economics is building models that better reflect actual behavior. Such behavior can be both rational and intelligent without being economy, related to this, behavioral economists and economic psychologists run experiments and engage to determine the choices people make and how these choices are made, and to asscertain to what extent from conventional economic wisedom.

Some important aspects on efficiency wages, efficient market hypothesis,social and personal captial, capabilities and soft, modification of economy theory does not suggest that relative prices, opportunity costs and incomes play no role in affected behavior, material incentives matter, supply and demand analysis is enriched by the findings, and methodology of behavioral economics, introducing effort variability, non-material variables, capabilities and relative positioning enriches production theory.

In businessmen profit earn aik vire, they can also apply behavioral economic theory to seek rationally to maximize, their rxpected , returns and had full knowledge of the data needed to
succeed in this attempt, they knew the relevant cost and demand functions, calculated marginal cost and marginal revenue from all actions open to them, and pushed each line of action to the point at which the relevant marginal cost and marginal revenue were equal. Hence, for example, it is not by learning and applying appropriate mathematical formulas that one becomes and
expert or decision maker, bur rather by developing the required skills. often learned in the pool hall and in the firm through learning -by-doing. A training program for firm decision making players, concentrating on math and engineering courses would by itself, not produce experts. Thus, behavioral assumptions should need to assume for optimal or rational intelligent choice behavior. Moreover, there exists a variety of non-profit maximizing behaviors that have a positive probability of never failing. In fact, it has shown that firms that maximize profits are the least likely to be the market survivors.

Hence, in different firms behavioral view, this sensitivity of outcomes to process can have important consequences for analysis at the level of market and economy, which assumes that consumer individual typically makes choices in their own best interest, " were best interest" is something that not incorporating into their calculations, the true costs and benefits of their choices.

Hence, behavioral economy theory can help product sellers to predict consumer individual choice , attitude in order to find what the important factors influence they choose to buy the seller's products in preference. Also, behavioral economic theory is an analytical predictions, how intelligent individuals actually behave. This approach to choice behavior does not assume that individuals are in any way irrational , even through such behavior is expected to deviate substantively. Hence, the behavioral economic theory assumes humans are rational and maximum their individual self interest.

In consumption view, in general , consumers choose to buy any products in preference, they will evaluate whether the product can bring the maximum economic or useful benefit to them in order to make the final purchase in our society. Such as organic food choice case, food consumers' choices , where people's may come from direct influence of other people's behavior and social norms on our behaviors. Then, theory assumes we independently know what we want and that our preferences are fixed. So, this standard theory is very good at explaining short -term decision-making. Suc as green vegatables and choose beans as they are on special offer, but can not explain longer-term changes in preferences. I now only choose organic foods. So, behavioral economy theory can predict short term consumers behavioral choice to decide what factors influence their choices change, but it can not predict long-term consumers behavioral choice to decide what factors influence their choices change, because it has much unpredictable factors are difficult to estimate , when they will influence now consumers behavioral change in our society.

Artificial intelligence is one good machine tool to predict consumer behavior in behavioral view, our social media, facebook, which is the most populat platform in the wourld. Any digital markets can apply webs, such as facebook to post message to communicate with their fans or followers (predicting online purchase behaviors , when they can occur). So, the applications of such method an be observed from data analysis in social media platforms to predict online consumers behaviors. Machine learning aims to maximize the efficiency of computer program using sample data or precedent experiences . A model is developed with designed in learning to perform computer program operation in order to enhance efficiency of the model using train data or post experiences. The model is developed to be capable of predicting or describing knowledge from the data or both. Hence, AI may be used to research consumer behavior probability from marketing communication by social medial web, face book online channel, on facebook using machine learning. Machine learning data classification to reseach consumer behavioral characteristicss to any kinds of product.

ON online purchase process research, online consumers must need to experience these five stages. They may include attention, interest, search, action adn share. In the beginning, working process starts when a consumer notices or sees a product, a service or an advertisement (attention). Then, the interest is stimulated in order to get more information about such product or service (search). In this stage, a consumer will seek for the others' comments, reviews, posts from internet, comparison websites, formal webpages of organization or even from a conversation with family members or friends who have been using the product or service. After that, the consumer will express whose own opinion considering the others' opinions on that product or service. This stage leads to the decision of the consumer to buy (action). Finally, the consumer will act as a messager by word of mouth, conversation, or online posts of whose opinion and impression (sharing). Thus, it seems that facebook pages may influence upon consumer behavior. When marketers who posses Facebook account to test. The messages posted through Facebook pages are then collected so as too through Facebook pages are then collected so as to perform a study of online consumer behaviors.

In fact, Facebook comprises of two main functions , which are the posting of message brands wish to communicate to consumers and opinions and comments of consumers responding to brand communication. It is one social media analysis tool tends to carry out the studies and analysis of consumer opinion with data collected from comment. The results measure consumer sentiment towards the product or service in form of positive, negative and neutial opinion.

Why is Facebook social medial terchnology more efficient to predict consumer behavior? This is due to the fact of the differences in business operation pattern and communication methods of each page. For example, page a puts focus on interaction with customers by organizing activities that customers can join. On the other hand, page is emphasizes an awareness rising to promote product to be known and understood, whereas page (stimulates customers to make a decision to buy the products). It is one good technological social media method to gather online consumer behaviors in biuying decision. After verifying posted messages, consumers seek for information from various sources prior to buy products and services, and they evaluate and reflect their satisfaction after buying products
and services. Online social media exercise greater influence that consumers can search for all concerned information , gather data from existing customers as much as possible before making a decision to buy. They do not need to meet the others and ask for their opinion towards product and service. IN addition, they can leave their opinion, impression and share information
to others as well. This illustrates prefectly online consumer behavior in decision making process to buy.

How to apply behavioral economic theory to evaluate household electricity useful decision making ? How to evaluate and explain adoption of energy efficiency between environment protection electricity energy household users and non-environment protection electricity household users for household solar, electricity, solar hot water and in-house energy. Their energy useful behaviors are influenced whether by either climate changing factor or other factors? It aims to apply behavioral economic theory to test and

explain their differences between high and low adopters of energy efficiency by macro-level factors (e.g. technological , economic, demographic factors) and an individual's perceptions, preferences and abilities, and cold or hot climate changing factors.

ON conclusion, ON behavioral economy view, in general, it concludes that householders feel need to save energy. The main reason may include this, due to the environment protection

energy users feel the tend to occur in the future when they concern discounting investments over long periods of time, which makes it is difficult to bring financial costs with respect to energy efficiency investments, as when they feel electricity energy cost will increase. They feel the energy use into total consumption will have much share to allocate to their whole families expenditure consumption. So, their energy useful or consumption psychological pressure influence these householder decide to use less energy and become their energy useful habits. So, it is not the the householder's psychological factor,whether the family is environment protection or non-environment protection energy users. So, this would provide the environment protection or non-environment protection householder energy users have a better sense of what scale of energy efficiency is achievable,thereby enabling them to reduce much extra householder whole family expenditure. Hence, these expenditure factor will influence many householders electricity energy useful behaviors as well as it can cause their energy useful habits and staying short time at home because they hope to avoid to spend much time to use energy at home. So, behavioral economy theory explains that environment protection factor is not the main factor to influence hosueholders energy consumption behavioral change.

9 798885 695794

Printed by Libri Plureos GmbH in Hamburg, Germany